1

JUNIOR

CLASSICS

Published in Red Turtle by
Rupa Publications India Pvt. Ltd 2016
7/16, Ansari Road, Daryaganj
New Delhi 110002

Sales centres:
Allahabad Bengaluru Chennai
Hyderabad Jaipur Kathmandu
Kolkata Mumbai

ISBN: 978-81-291-3885-9

Second impression 2017

10 9 8 7 6 5 4 3 2

Printed at Rakmo Press Pvt. Ltd, New Delhi

Contents

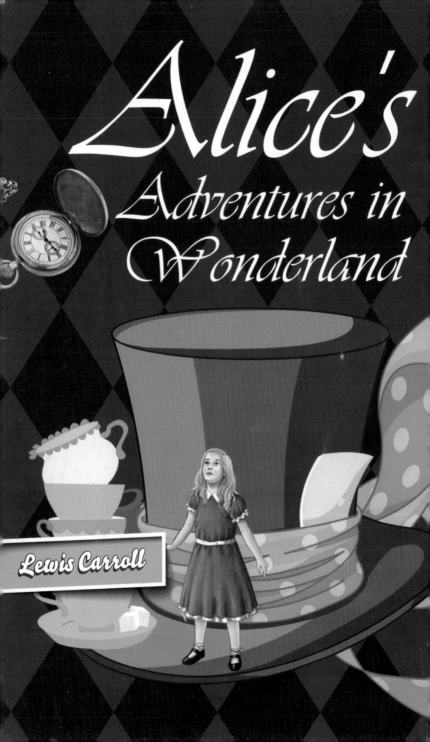

Alice's
Adventures in
Wonderland

Lewis Carroll

Alice was beginning to get very tired of sitting by her sister on the bank and of having nothing to do while her sister read. Suddenly, a White Rabbit with pink eyes ran by her and she heard it say,

'Oh dear! I shall be late!'

Alice should have found it strange, but she did not. However, when the rabbit took out a watch from its waistcoat, Alice wondered if she had ever seen a rabbit with a watch and a waistcoat before. Burning with curiosity, she ran after it only to see it pop down a large rabbit hole.

The next moment, Alice jumped into the rabbit hole, without considering how she would come back. The tunnel was very long and very dark.

'How long I have been falling!' Alice exclaimed. 'I must be falling to the centre of the Earth!'

When Alice finally hit the ground, it did not hurt at all.

Alice looked up and saw the White Rabbit hurrying down the passage. Alice followed him around a bend, and found herself in a big hall full of locked doors. To her great surprise, the White Rabbit had vanished!

She looked around and saw a tiny golden key on a glass table. 'Aha! This must open one of the doors,' she thought. Sadly, the key did not fit any of the locks. She then came across a tiny door, hidden behind a curtain. The key fit the lock perfectly. The door opened onto a small passage. Alice bent down and saw the loveliest garden outside. Oh, how she wanted to go out! 'If only I could fold up like a telescope,' she thought. She went back to the hall, hoping to find another key. Instead, she found a bottle labelled 'Drink Me'.

Alice first checked to see if the bottle was marked 'poison'. Being smart, she knew that contents of bottles marked 'poison' generally disagreed with you. Satisfied with her scrutiny, Alice took a sip from the bottle. She quite liked the flavour—a mixture of cherry tart, custard, pineapple, roast turkey, toffee and hot buttered toast—and soon emptied the bottle.

'What a curious feeling!' said Alice, 'I must be folding up.'

And so she was. Now, she was only ten inches tall, and could easily fit through a fifteen-inch garden door. She decided to wait few minutes just to see if she would shrink any further. When nothing happened, poor Alice went to the small door, but she had forgotten the little golden key!

Alice went back to get it, but she was too small now. She could see the key, but could not reach it—not even if she tried to climb the slippery legs of the table.

Tired of trying, the poor child sat down and started crying.

'There's no use in crying like that!' she scolded herself, 'I advise you to stop crying right now!'

She generally gave herself very good advice (which she sometimes even followed) and sometimes scolded herself so harshly as to bring tears to her eyes.

Her eyes then fell on a little glass box under the table. She opened it and found a small cake labelled 'Eat Me'. She decided to eat the cake. 'If it makes me grow larger, I can reach the key, and if it makes me shrink, I can creep under the door. Either way, I can get into the garden,' she thought.

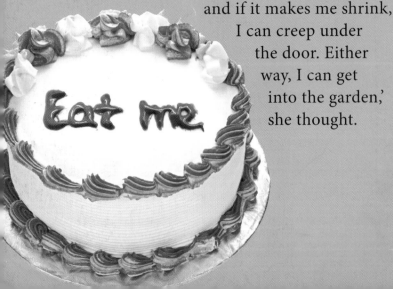

She nibbled at the cake curious to see what would happen. Nothing happened. A very disappointed Alice ate the entire cake.

'Curiouser and curiouser! Now I am opening out like a telescope!' she said, for she had started growing rapidly.

'Goodbye, feet!' she said, for she could not even see her feet when she looked down. Soon her head hit the roof and she was now nine feet tall. At once, she took the key and rushed to the door.

Poor Alice! All she could do was lie on her side and look at the garden through the window with one eye. She began to cry and shed gallons of tears. Soon there was a large pool all round her, about four inches deep and reaching halfway down the hall.

After some time, she heard a pattering of little feet in the distance. She hastily dried her eyes and saw the White Rabbit returning, splendidly dressed, with a pair of white kid gloves in one hand and a large fan in the other. He was hurrying along, muttering, 'Oh! The Duchess, the Duchess! Oh! Won't she be savage if I've kept her waiting!'

Alice was desperate. When the White Rabbit came near her, she began, in a timid voice, 'If you please, sir…'

The startled White Rabbit dropped his gloves and the fan and ran away into the darkness as fast as he could. Alice picked up the fan and gloves. The hall was very hot, so she fanned herself, talking all the while.

'Oh, dear! How strange this is! Have I changed into someone else? But if I'm not me, who am I?'

She then began to think of all the children she knew, who were of the same age as herself, to see if she could have been changed into any of them.

'I'm sure I'm not Ada,' she said, 'for her hair falls in such long ringlets, and mine does not. And I'm sure I can't be Mabel, for I know all sorts of things, and she knows so little!'

'Besides,' she went on, 'she's she, and I'm I, and—oh dear, how puzzling this is! I'll try to see if I know all the things I used to know. Let's try Geography. London is the capital of Paris, and Paris is the capital of Rome and Rome—no, that's all wrong, I'm certain! I must have changed into Mabel!' And her eyes filled with tears again.

She looked down at her hands and was surprised to see that she had put on one of the White Rabbit's gloves while she was talking. She thought, 'I must be growing small again.'

She was shrinking rapidly. She soon realized this was because of the fan she was holding, and she dropped it hastily.

'That was a narrow escape!' said Alice frightened that she might have shrunk altogether.

To her dismay, Alice realized that she had again forgotten the key! Suddenly her foot slipped and she fell in a pool of salt water.

For a moment she was sure it was the sea, but then realized they were her tears. Alice heard splashing; she looked around and saw a mouse swimming nearby.

'Oh Mouse, do you know the way out of this pool?' she asked.

When the Mouse did not reply, she decided he must be French. She recited the first sentence from her French lesson-book: '*Ou est ma chatte?*'

The Mouse looked around, terrified.

Alice had just asked, 'Where is my cat?'

'Oh! I beg your pardon, I forgot you don't like cats,' she said.

'Would you like cats, if you were me?' asked the Mouse.

Alice apologized, but insisted that the Mouse would like Dinah, if he met her.

'She sits purring so nicely by the fire,' Alice said, 'and she is such an expert on catching mice—oh, I beg your pardon!'

The Mouse bristled at this and called cats 'nasty, low, vulgar things'.

Wanting to change the topic, Alice said, 'There is such a nice little dog near our house I should like to show you! A little bright-eyed terrier, with long curly brown hair! The farmer who owns it says it sits up and begs for its dinner, and it kills all the rats and—oh dear!'

The Mouse swam away. Alice apologized again, and promised not to talk about cats or dogs, and the Mouse promised to tell her why he hated cats and dogs as soon as they were ashore.

Soon, other creatures—including a Duck, a Dodo, a Lory and an Eaglet—joined them in the pool which quickly became crowded. When Alice eventually led them all to the shore, they were all dripping wet, cold and cross.

They tried to decide how to get dry again. Alice and Lory got into an argument, which went on until the Mouse intervened with a solution.

'Sit down and listen to me, I'll soon make you dry enough' and everyone sat around the Mouse as it started a long, and rather dry story about William the Conqueror.

After a while, the Mouse asked Alice, 'How are you getting on now, my dear?'

'As wet as ever,' said Alice in a melancholy tone, 'your story does not seem to be working at all.'

The Dodo suggested a solution, 'The best thing to get us dry would be a Caucus-race.'

'What is a Caucus-race?' asked Alice.

'The best way to explain it is to do it,' said the Dodo, marking out a sort of circle to serve as a race course.

All the members of their party stood at random points inside the circle. There was no signal to start the race, and everyone ran around however, and whenever they felt like it. It was all very confusing! However, soon they were all dry.

Dodo abruptly called the race to an end. Everyone huddled around him asking who had won.

'Everyone's a winner,' said the Dodo.

He then demanded that Alice give out the prizes. Luckily, she had a few sweets with her which she distributed among them.

After a while, everyone settled down to listen to the Mouse's story of why he hated cats and dogs.

'Mine is a long and a sad tale,' he said.

'It is a long tail, certainly,' said Alice, looking down with wonder at the Mouse's tail, 'but why do you call it sad?'

The story did not make sense to Alice, and she was distracted. This annoyed the Mouse, and he left.

All the creatures wished it would come back.

'If only Dinah were here,' Alice said wistfully, 'she would have brought the Mouse back.'

'Who is Dinah?' they all wanted to know.

Alice, in her excitement, told them all about her cat and how good she was at catching mice and birds. This had a remarkable effect on the party and everyone hurried home under some pretext or the other. Poor Alice was once again all alone.

Soon she heard shuffling of feet at some distance and eagerly looked up, half hoping it to be the Mouse.

It was the White Rabbit looking anxiously about as it went, muttering, 'The Duchess! Oh my fur and whiskers! She'll have me executed! Where can I have dropped them, I wonder?'

Alice guessed it was looking for the fan and the pair of white gloves, and Alice started looking for them immediately. But the hall had changed completely since her swim in the pool. There was no glass table or door to be found! Soon the White Rabbit saw Alice and mistaking her for his maid servant said, 'Quick, Mary Ann, run home and fetch me a pair of gloves and a fan!'

Alice quickly ran away in the direction wondering, how the White Rabbit would react when he found out who she really was.

She soon came upon a house with 'W. RABBIT' engraved on the door plate. Alice entered without knocking and up she went lest someone find her. She found herself in a room where the fan and gloves were kept on the table. Alice was about to leave when her eyes fell on a bottle. Curious to know what would happen this time, she drank from it.

When nothing happened, she drank some more and then suddenly she started growing! She curled on the floor and still kept growing. Her elbow was blocking the door, another arm was stretched out of the window and her leg was up in the chimney!

The White Rabbit soon came searching for the gloves and fan. But when he tried entering the room Alice's elbow kept blocking it. He tried climbing in through the window, but Alice's huge arm drove him away. The White Rabbit and his servants tried many ways to get in, but could not. When the gardener, Bill the Lizard tried to come through the chimney, she kicked him away! Fed up, they threw rocks at her. These hit her everywhere and, strangely, turned into cakes as soon as they came into the house! Alice guessed—correctly—that they would make her small again if she ate them.

Afraid of the mob outside the White Rabbit's house, Alice ran towards the woods. She had never been more unsure about what to eat. Alice made a neat little plan: she had to grow up to her right size again and then find her way to the garden and she knew that to grow up to her right size she must eat something. The great question was what to eat.

Soon Alice found herself in front of a large mushroom almost as tall as she was. Her eyes locked in on those of a large blue caterpillar who was sitting on top of it, smoking a hookah.

'Who are you?' the Caterpillar asked.

Poor Alice had gone through so many changes that she was no longer sure who she was.

'It's very confusing,' she said.

'No, it's not,' said the Caterpillar.

'Maybe it isn't yet,' Alice said, 'but when you have to turn into a chrysalis, and then into a butterfly, I should think you'll feel it a little queer, won't you?'

'Not a bit,' the Caterpillar said.

'Maybe it's different for you,' Alice said, 'but it's very weird for me.'

'You!' said the Caterpillar contemptuously. 'Who are you?'

Which brought them back again to the beginning of the conversation. Alice felt a little irritated at the Caterpillar's rude behaviour and turned away.

'Come back!' the Caterpillar called after her, 'I have something important to say!'

Intrigued, Alice came back to the caterpillar. It asked her to recite a poem, even though she did not remember it. Then, when Alice said she would like to be a little taller, since three inches was a wretched height, the Caterpillar got offended. It was exactly three inches tall.

The Caterpillar ignored her for a while and began to crawl away. As it left, it remarked, 'One side will make you taller, and the other side will make you shorter.'

'One side of what? The other side of what?' Alice thought.

'Of the mushroom,' said the Caterpillar, answering her thought.

She nibbled a small piece from the right-hand side, and began shrinking rapidly! Frightened, she tried a bit from the other side. Her neck shot up, zigzagging far above her shoulders, towards the treetops. Unfortunately, a pigeon mistook Alice's neck for a snake and attacked her to protect its eggs. Alice had to work hard to convince the stubborn pigeon that she was not a snake.

Alice nibbled on the mushroom till she was the correct size. 'Now that one part of the plan is done, I must find the garden,' she said.

As she said this, she came suddenly upon an open place, with a little house in it about four feet high. Quickly, she nibbled on the right side of the mushroom and was nine inches tall.

She was wondering what to do, when a footman—who looked like a fish—came running and knocked on the door. Another footman, who looked like a frog, opened the door.

Alice peeked out of the woods to see what was happening. Fish-Footman had taken out a letter, almost as large as himself, and handed it over to Frog-Footman, saying, 'From the Queen: an invitation for the Duchess to play croquet.'

Frog-Footman took the letter and repeated, 'From the Queen: An invitation for the Duchess to play croquet.' Alice burst out laughing at this, and hid behind some trees so they would not hear her.

When Alice went up to the door, she saw the Frog-Footman sitting alone looking at the sky. She tried to talk to him but he kept talking nonsense, so she ignored him and went inside. She found herself in a large and smoky kitchen. The Duchess was sitting on a three-legged stool in the middle, nursing a baby; the cook, it seemed, was preparing soup.

Alice sneezed violently and thought, 'There's certainly too much pepper in that soup!' Even the Duchess was sneezing occasionally and the baby was constantly sneezing and howling alternately. Only the cook and the large cat—which was sitting and grinning from ear to ear—were not sneezing. Alice had never seen any cat grin, and asked the Duchess about it.

The Duchess told her it was a Cheshire Cat and then pointed out that Alice did not know much about anything.

Insulted, Alice tried to change the topic. Just then, the cook took the soup off the fire, and started throwing everything within reach—saucepans, plates and dishes—at the Duchess and the baby.

The Duchess ignored the missiles, even when they hit her and the baby! She kept nursing it, singing a weird lullaby and bouncing the baby violently while she sang.

'Please, mind what you're doing!' said Alice in terror.

The Duchess flung the baby at her, saying, 'Here! You nurse it! I must go and get ready to play croquet with the Queen.'

She hurried out of the room. Alice caught the baby with some difficulty. It grunted. Alice did not know what to do with the baby and was wondering aloud whether it would be safe if she left it behind.

The baby grunted again. So Alice said, 'Don't grunt, it's not proper.'

She thought the baby looked a little like a pig, so she stared at it for a while. Then she realized the baby was a pig! She let the creature down and it trotted off into the woods.

The Cheshire Cat was grinning at her from the bough of a nearby tree.

Alice was startled at first, but later asked the Cat, 'Would you tell me, please, which way I ought to go from here?'

'That depends on where you want to go,' said the Cat.

'I don't really care where—,' said Alice.

'Then it doesn't matter which way you go,' said the Cat.

'—so long as I get somewhere,' Alice added as an explanation.

'Oh, you're sure to do that,' said the Cat, 'if you only walk long enough.'

'In that direction lives a Hatter,' the Cat said, waving its right paw. Waving its other paw, it said, 'In that direction, lives a March Hare. Visit whichever one you like. They're both mad.'

'But I don't want to visit mad people,' Alice said.

'Oh, you can't help that,' said the Cat, 'we're all mad here. I'm mad. You're mad.'

'How do you know I'm mad?' Alice asked.

'You must be, or you wouldn't come here,' the Cat said and vanished, saying it would see her at the Queen's croquet game.

Alice was shocked to see that the Cat's grin shimmered in the air long after its owner had disappeared.

Alice decided to visit the March Hare. His house had ear-shaped chimneys and the roof was thatched with fur.

The March Hare and the Hatter were having a tea party in front of the house. A Dormouse was fast asleep between them. They were all crowded around one corner of the large table and, when they saw Alice, they shouted, 'No room! No room!'

'There's plenty of room,' Alice said, and sat down in a large arm-chair.

There was only tea on the table, but the March Hare offered Alice wine. Alice angrily told him he should not offer her something he did not have.

'You shouldn't have sat down without an invitation,' he said.

The Hatter told Alice she needed a haircut, and she told him he was rude.

The Hatter's eyes opened wide at this, but all he said was, 'Why is a raven like a writing desk?'

Alice was glad that they had moved on to riddles, but they quickly began arguing about meaning what one said and saying what one meant.

After a while, the Hatter asked Alice, 'What day of the month is it?'

He was shaking his watch and holding it to his ear uneasily. When Alice answered him, he said, 'Two days wrong!' He turned to the March Hare angrily. 'I told you not to use butter!'

'It was the best butter,' the March Hare replied meekly.

'Yes, but some crumbs must have got in as well,' the Hatter grumbled, 'you shouldn't have put it in with the bread-knife.'

'Have you guessed the riddle yet?' the Hatter said, turning to Alice again.

Alice did not know and asked for the answer.

'I haven't the slightest idea,' the Hatter said.

When Alice told him he should not waste time with random riddles, he informed her that Time was a he, not an it. Hatter told her he had been friends with Time once, but they had quarrelled the previous year, at the Queen's concert.

'I was singing,' Hatter said, and started singing:

Twinkle, twinkle, little bat!
How I wonder what you're at!
Up above the world you fly,
Like a tea-tray in the sky.

'Anyway,' he went on, 'I'd hardly finished the first verse, when the Queen jumped up and yelled, "He's murdering time! Off with his head!" Ever since then, it's always tea-time. I don't even have time to wash the cups!'

The Dormouse soon started telling a story about three girls who lived in a well, ate treacle and learnt to draw. Alice kept interrupting, because it was a confusing story.

He asked if she had ever seen a drawing of muchness.

Alice began, 'I don't think…'

The Hatter interrupted her, saying, 'Then you shouldn't talk.'

Alice was offended by this rudeness and decided to leave the party and never return.

She soon found a tree with a door leading right inside it and went in.

Alice found herself back in the hall. She took the little golden key and, after nibbling on the mushroom to get down to the right size, went through the door, into the lovely garden.

There was a rose tree near the entrance. The roses were white, but three gardeners—named Five, Seven and Two—were busy painting them red. Two told Alice that, instead of red roses, they had planted white roses by mistake. So they were painting them all red before the Queen got there. He had hardly finished talking when the Queen was announced. All three of them fell flat upon their faces to greet the Queen.

First came ten soldiers carrying clubs. Like the gardeners, they were oblong and flat, their hands and feet at the corners. Then came the ten courtiers; these were ornamented all over with diamonds. After these came the royal children— ten of them, all ornamented with Hearts.

Next came the guests, mostly Kings and Queens, and among them Alice recognized the White Rabbit. Then followed the Knave of Hearts, carrying the King's crown on a crimson velvet cushion and last of all this grand procession came the King and Queen of Hearts.

When the procession was in front of Alice, they all stopped and looked at her, and the Queen said severely, 'Who is this?'

She said it to the Knave of Hearts, who only bowed and smiled in reply.

'My name is Alice, so please your Majesty,' said Alice very politely; but she added, to herself, 'Why, they're only a pack of cards, after all. I needn't be afraid of them!'

The Queen did see what the gardeners had been doing and ordered their execution but Alice hid them and saved their lives.

The Queen asked, 'Can you play croquet?' The question seemed to be obviously meant for Alice.

'Yes!' said Alice.

'Come on, then!' roared the Queen.

'It's—it's a very fine day!' said a timid

voice at her side. She was walking by the White Rabbit, who was peeping anxiously into her face.

'Very,' said Alice, '—where's the Duchess?'

'Hush! Hush!' said the White Rabbit in a low, hurried tone. He looked anxiously over his shoulder as he spoke, raised himself upon tiptoe, put his mouth close to her ear, and whispered, 'She's under sentence of execution.'

'What for?' said Alice.

'She boxed the Queen's ears—,' the White Rabbit began.

'Get to your places!' said the Queen in a voice of thunder, and people began running about in all directions, tumbling up against each other.

However, they settled down in a minute or two, and the game began.

Alice thought she had never seen such a curious croquet ground in her life—it was all ridges and furrows.

The balls were live hedgehogs, the mallets, live flamingos, and the soldiers had to double themselves up and to stand on their hands and feet to make the arches. The players all played at once without waiting for turns, quarrelling all the while and fighting for the hedgehogs; and in a very short time the Queen was in a furious passion, and went stamping about, and shouting 'Off with his head!' or 'Off with her head!' about once every minute.

'They're dreadfully fond of beheading people here; the great wonder is that there's any one left alive!' thought Alice.

She was looking about for some way of escape when she noticed a grinning mouth hovering in the air. 'It's the Cheshire Cat: now I shall have somebody to talk to,' Alice thought.

'How are you getting on?' said the Cat.

'I don't think they play at all fairly,' Alice said, in rather a complaining tone, 'and they all quarrel so dreadfully one can't hear oneself speak—and they don't seem to have any rules.'

Alice thought she might as well go back (she had already heard the Queen sentence three players). So she went in search of the hedgehog, by the time she returned to the Cat, she was surprised to see a large crowd around it. The King did not like the Cat, and the Queen sentenced him to death. However, the Cheshire Cat remained invisible—except for his floating head—and the executioner refused to carry out the sentence.

'I've never executed a head without a body, and I'm not about to start now,' he said.

Alice suggested that the Cat belonged to the Duchess. However, by the time the Duchess came on the scene, the Cat had disappeared completely.

The Duchess seemed in a very good mood. She even linked her arm to Alice's and talked about finding morals in everything that happened. She was so intimate with Alice that the poor girl was scared of her. The Duchess was still talking when her voice died away and her arm began to tremble.

Alice looked up, and there stood the Queen in front of them, frowning like a thunderstorm.

'Now, I give you fair warning,' said the Queen, stamping on the ground as she spoke, 'either you or your head must be off, and that in about half no time! Take your choice!'

The Duchess was gone in a moment.

'Let's go on with the game,' the Queen said to Alice; too frightened to say a word, she slowly followed the Queen back.

The entire time, the Queen ordered executions and by the end only the Queen, the King and Alice were left.

The Queen asked Alice to come along to visit the Mock Turtle, who would tell her his story. As they walked off together, Alice heard the King say in a low voice, to the company generally, 'You are all pardoned.' The Queen told the Gryphon to take Alice to the Mock Turtle. He told Alice that no one ever got executed.

'It's all her fancy, that,' he said.

They soon reached the Mock Turtle; sitting sad and lonely on a rock. The Mock Turtle told Alice all about his sea-school where they learnt subjects like: Reeling, Writhing, Ambition, Distraction, Uglyfication and Derision. Alice found these subjects very strange!

The Mock Turtle then told her about a type of dance called the Lobster Quadrille.

Having no experience of the lobster, apart from the one time she tasted one, Alice was excited to learn all about the dance. Not only did the Turtle explain the dance to Alice, he and the Gryphon even gave her a demonstration, too.

Then they made her tell them her adventures and even repeat one of her lessons, which confused them thoroughly.

A cry of 'The trial's beginning!' was heard in the distance, and they all began to run towards the trial.

'What trial is it?' Alice panted as she ran, but the Gryphon only answered, 'Come on!' and ran faster.

The King and Queen were already seated when they reached. All the creatures had gathered—all the birds and animals, the whole pack of cards, everyone. The Knave of Hearts was standing in chains; the White Rabbit with the trumpet and a scroll was there too. Twelve creatures—animals and birds—were in the jury box.

The accusation was this:

'The Queen of Hearts, she made some tarts,

All on a summer day:

The Knave of Hearts, he stole those tarts,

And took them quite away!'

The first witness to be called was the Hatter.

Poor Hatter had come along with his tea and bread-butter as he had not managed to finish his tea!

The King asked, 'When did you start the tea?'

'On the 14th of March,' the Hatter said.

Poor Hatter was so nervous he trembled all over. He muddled everything he was saying.

The King said, 'Don't be nervous

or I shall have you executed!' which wasn't very helpful. All he could manage to say after that was 'I… I'm a poor man… I am just a Hatter…'

'You are a very poor speaker,' said the Queen while examining the list of last year's singers. The Hatter scampered away as soon as the next witness, the Duchess' cook, was called.

She trotted to the witness box with her box of pepper and everyone in the court started sneezing! She refused to give witness and managed to disappear in the commotion that ensued.

Alice had started to grow at a rapid rate, and to her great surprise she was the next witness!

'Here!' said Alice.

In her haste, Alice forgot how much Alice had grown and in her hurry she managed to upset the entire jury box, with the jury members toppled on one another.

'The trial cannot proceed until all the jurymen are in their proper places.'

'What do you know about this business?' the King said to Alice.

'Nothing whatever,' said Alice.

'That's very important,' said the King. Turning to the jury the White Rabbit interrupted,

'Unimportant, your Majesty means, of course,' he said in a very respectful tone.

'Unimportant, of course, I meant,' the King hastily said. Some of the jury wrote down 'important,' and some 'unimportant'.

At this moment the King, who was busy writing in his book, read out from it, 'Rule Forty-two. All persons more than a mile high to leave the court.'

Everybody looked at Alice.

'I'm not a mile high,' said Alice.

'Nearly two miles high,' said the Queen.

'Well, I shan't go, at any rate,' said Alice, 'besides, that's not a regular rule: you invented it just now.'

Confused, the King shut his book and asked the jurymen for their verdict.

The White Rabbit hurried, 'But there is more evidence! This letter has been just picked up. It was written by the prisoner.'

It was not a letter after all, but a set of unsigned, nonsensical verses.

The Knave begged, 'I did not write it, Your Majesty!'

The verses were read out. They made no sense. Alice declared, 'I don't believe it!'

Now that she was larger than them, she was no longer afraid of the King and the Queen. However, the King showed the court how the verses proved the Knave guilty.

The King asked for the jurymen's verdict but the Queen interrupted, 'No, no. Sentence first, verdict later.'

'Stuff and nonsense, the idea of having the sentence first!' said Alice.

'How dare you?' said the Queen turning purple with anger. 'Off with her head! Off with her head!'

Nobody moved.

'I am not scared of you,' said Alice, now grown to her full height. 'You are just a pack of cards!'

At this, the whole pack attacked her: she gave a little scream, and tried to beat them off, and found herself lying on the bank, with her head in the lap of her sister, who was gently brushing away some dead leaves that had fluttered down from the trees upon her face.

'Wake up, Alice dear!' said her sister, 'Why, what a long sleep you've had!'

'Oh, I've had such a curious dream!' said Alice.

She told her sister all these strange adventures of hers that you have just been reading about; and when she had finished, her sister said, 'It was a curious dream, dear, certainly, but now have your tea; it's getting late.'

So Alice got up and ran off to have her tea. But her sister sat still, thinking of little Alice and all her wonderful adventures, till she too began dreaming.

What Katy Did

Susan Coolidge

One day, when I was sitting by the meadow, two small voices began disputing something. One said, 'Katy did,' and the other said, 'Katy didn't'. They must have repeated those two words at least a hundred times.

I got up to look for the speakers and noticed two tiny, pale-green insects on one of the bulrushes. When I was there, they did not say anything, but the moment I turned my back, they began to quarrel again and utter the same words.

On my way home, I started thinking about another Katy I once knew. She planned to do many wonderful things and in the end did something quite different instead. Here is her story, named in honour of my little green friends: the story of What Katy Did.

Twelve-year-old Katy Carr lived in Burnet, in a large house on the edge of the town with her three younger sisters and two younger brothers.

Clover was next in age to Katy. She was a sweet girl with light brown hair and short-sighted blue eyes. Next was eight-year-old Elsie, a thin child with beautiful dark eyes. She longed to go about with Katy, Clover and Cecy Hall, who lived next door. However, the older girls made her play with the little children.

Then came Dorry and Joanna. Dorry was a pale, pudgy six-year-old boy, while Joanna— whom the children called 'John,' and 'Johnnie'— was a square, splendid girl, a year younger than Dorry. Phil, the littlest, was four years old.

Their father, Dr Carr (the children addressed him as Papa) was a kind, busy man, who spent most of his time away from home, taking care of sick people. The children's mother died when Phil was a baby. Of all her siblings, only Katy could remember her. Papa's sister, old Aunt Izzie, took care of the children. Aunt Izzie meant to be kind to them, but she just could not understand them.

One day, the five younger ones were sitting together in the yard, waiting for Katy to finish her chores. They were planning to visit 'Paradise', a marshy thicket near their home which to them was an endless forest in a fairy land.

It was their first visit to Paradise since winter. It did not take long for them to reach their favourite picnic spot, which was a very small bower, which could only take the children, the baskets and the kitten.

Katy opened the basket, which had many ginger cakes, buttered biscuits, a dozen hard-boiled eggs and thick corn beef sandwiches.

After finishing their meal, they decided to play a game where they spoke what they would be when they were grown up.

Cecy said she would be a pretty woman, who taught in Sunday school and visited the poor.

'Pooh!' said Clover. 'I'm going to be the most

beautiful woman in the world. And I'm going to live in a yellow castle with a pond full of perfume.'

'Me too!' cried Elsie, excited by this gorgeous vision. 'Only, my pond will be the biggest. I shall be a great deal beautifuller, too,' she added.

Johnnie did not have any particular plans, but Dorry's were very clear: he wanted to have turkey every day, and lots of pudding.

Katy said she wanted to be beautiful and as good as she could be; she wanted a big house, where the children would live with her and play in the garden every day. She also said she would do grand things.

Eventually, Johnnie and Dorry trotted off together.

Then, Katy said she had found Dorry's journal and she would show it to them if they promised not to tell anyone. They promised, and Katy read the entries from the journal—all one-liners, and mainly about food. They laughed.

It soon became dark and they packed up, not wanting to leave but comforted in knowing that Paradise would always be there.

Katy and Cecy went to Mrs Knight's school. Miller's school was next door. The schools' playgrounds were separated by a fence, through which the 'Knights' and the 'Millerites' constantly fought and made faces at each other. One morning, Katy could not find her algebra book, her slate, and her bonnet string. Aunt Izzie located her book and bonnet string, but made Katy wait while she sewed the string back on, and so Katy was late.

That day all things went wrong for Katy. As soon as the bell rang, she ran outside and climbed the roof of the shed to be alone. As she sat, a gust of wind blew her bonnet off into Mrs Miller's yard.

Katy watched in horror, thinking of the terrible things the Millerites would do with her bonnet. So, she vaulted over the fence to retrieve it.

Just then, Mrs Miller's bell rang, and Millerites came pouring out. Seeing Katy in their yard, they furiously descended upon her. Katy quickly climbed back over the fence, into a group of Knights who praised her bravery and made her tell them the story multiple times.

During the lunch break, Katy invented a new game called the Game of Rivers. Each girl pretended to be a river and ran across the room, making loud river noises. As Father Ocean, Katy growled and roared. The girls' racket drew a crowd to the school. When Mrs Knight returned from lunch, she rushed inside, anxious to see what the chaos was about.

When they heard Mrs Knight's voice, the girls fell quiet and felt guilty. Mrs Knight brought things to order and, as punishment, cancelled the girls' recess for three weeks.

Talking to Papa, that evening, Katy decided it was all because she had not sewed her bonnet string on earlier!

Mondays were always chaotic. Aunt Izzie and the servants seemed crosser than usual, and the children were very frisky after quiet Sundays.

On Saturday nights, Clover and Elsie had their hair screwed up in papers for it to curl on Sunday. Clover had straight hair, and the tight knobs and pins on her head bothered her.

Sundays began with a Bible story, followed by breakfast, Sunday school lessons, and then church. After church was Sunday school, then dinner. In the afternoon, Katy usually forced the children to listen while she read out a religious paper called *The Sunday Visitor* that she edited.

That rainy Monday, the children were cooped up in the nursery. Phil was unwell and had been taking a medicine called Elixir Pro. John wanted to give Pikery—a yellow chair she considered a doll—the medicine, so she took the Elixir Pro and poured it all over Pikery's seat! Aunt Izzie saw the mess and scolded John.

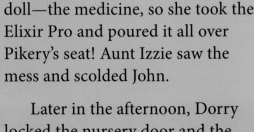

Later in the afternoon, Dorry locked the nursery door and the children could not open it again. They began to scream in fear and Aunt Izzie heard them and called someone to enter through the window and open the door from inside. They were quite thrilled at their daring rescue, but Aunt Izzie scolded them again. Katy missed the adventure since she was in the library.

As Katy came out, Aunt Izzie told her that she was going out, and that the children were to be in bed by nine. Aunt Izzie rarely went out, but when she did the children felt a sense of freedom.

Everything went peacefully, until after supper and lessons, when the children began to discuss Kikeri, a game they had invented. In Kikeri, all the children hide in a dark room, and one person searches for them. As this game resulted in broken toys and bruises, Aunt Izzie had banned it.

Now, however, they played it, and banged about the nursery. They lost track of time completely, till they heard the sound of the bus. Aunt Izzie was back!

The children rushed about, crawling into bed half-dressed. Clover panicked. She sat down in the nursery and began to pray.

Aunt Izzie found Clover like that and, after scolding her, sent her to bed. One by one, Aunt Izzie found the other children in bed with their clothes still on, and scolded them all (except Elsie who had fallen asleep). Katy felt terrible for setting such a bad example. The next day, Papa banned the game and talked to Katy seriously about her responsibilities.

'Do you remember Mama's wishes?' he asked. Katy nodded. Before she died, Mama had said, 'Katy must be a Mama to the little ones, when she grows up.'

'Do you think that, maybe, it is time you followed Mama's wishes?' he asked. Katy sobbed for hours, and although she made no promises, I think she was never quite so thoughtless again.

The next day, Miss Petingill was sitting in the little room doing her week's mending. She was a funny, lovable old woman who spent her days sewing. Her round face was puckered by a thousand lines and she was excellent at her work.

Suddenly, Miss Petingill saw the seven children stream out of the wood-house door—which was not a door, but a tall open arch, which gave way to a loft.

Katy, who was at the head, bore a large black bottle, while the others carried a cookie each. They went up a tall wooden post with spikes driven into it almost a foot apart, with Clover and Cecy boosting the little ones from behind.

Finally, they reached the low, dark loft. There were no windows. The only source of light was a hole in the floor. It was surrounded by cobwebs on the corner and wet spots on the floor. This was their favourite place to spend rainy Saturdays.

Katy commenced the fete (she pronounced it 'feet). After eating, they began to read aloud to each other. Cecy started with, 'A Tragedy of the Alhambra', a story about a knight who had just met Zuleika, the woman he was in love with.

Next was a 'Yap, a Simple Poem' by Clover, which received immense applause from all the children, followed by scripture verses by Elsie and Joanna. Last was Dorry, who recited a hymn. Then, they decided to have their feast.

Katy had many eccentric friendships. One was with their neighbour, Marianne, whom Katy decided to adopt. She and Clover persuaded Marianne to come home with them. They had a delightful time the whole day but, at night, after Katy and Clover were sent to bed, lonely Marianne began to scream in fright. Katy's father found her, and got to the bottom of things.

Katy's next, stranger friendship was with a bad-tempered, old, black woman, who lived near Katy's school. After this, Katy took a fancy to two pretty German twin sisters, and would give them flowers. There were other acquaintances—a cook, a bonnet maker, even a thief in the town jail!

The oddest of all of Katy's eccentric friends was the mysterious Mrs Spenser. She was an invalid and stayed alone most of the time. One day Katy found Mrs Spenser lying sick in the bedroom and gave her flowers. She visited her regularly thereafter. This stopped when Mrs Spenser's husband took her and disappeared one night. It turned out that Mr Spenser was a criminal, and the police wanted to arrest him.

Once, Katy asked Aunt Izzie for permission to invite Imogen Clark, a new girl in Katy's school, to spend Saturday with them. Aunt Izzie was not happy to let her come over. But Imogen was waiting just outside the gate, so Aunt Izzie said 'yes'.

The children were very excited about Imogen's visit. Imogen arrived dressed in fancy clothes, and dazzled the children. She behaved airy and grown-up and was not happy playing in the bower or the loft, or sitting outside and reciting poetry.

Instead, she wanted to sit in the dark parlour, which generally was Aunt Izzie's territory. Imogen seemed very comfortable there, and began telling Katy and Clover adventurous stories about herself.

Katy and Clover were so absorbed in her tales that they did not hear their father come home. They sat, oblivious, until Papa asked Aunt Izzie why they were in the parlour, and she called them out. Aunt Izzie scolded them, and Imogen told Katy she thought Aunt Izzie was not very nice. This offended Katy, and after dinner, they were all glad to see Imogen leave.

On the last day of school Aunt Izzie told the children, 'Your Cousin Helen is coming to visit us.'

The news excited Katy and Clover, to whom Cousin Helen was as unreal as anyone they had read about in fairy tales. None of them had ever met her before. The children knew that Cousin Helen was an invalid and required help at all times. They also knew she was very sweet and patient.

When she arrived, Cousin Helen was excited to see them and when Papa laid her on the hall sofa, he told the little ones, 'Cousin Helen wants to see you.'

Papa had taken Helen upstairs to the Blue-room to rest, while they had all gone out to play. Katy insisted she would help to take the tray upstairs, which was met with a firm 'no' from Aunt Izzie.

But Katy's eyes begged so hard that her Papa let her do so. However, when she reached the door of the Blue-room, she stumbled and Aunt Izzie scolded her immediately.

As Aunt Izzie prepared another tray, Cousin Helen pleaded, 'Please allow her to bring it up!' This time Katy was careful and placed the tray safely on the table. Cousin Helen was nicer than they had ever imagined!

The children woke up very early and went up to see Cousin Helen, white and tired, but her eyes and smile as bright as ever. Katy presented her with flowers and began talking to her.

Their Papa then entered, and wanted to have a word with Cousin Helen. Katy sat on the floor, holding Cousin Helen's hand and listened to her speak to Papa.

After dinner, Katy asked Papa about Alex, the person he and Helen had been talking about.

Papa hesitantly told Katy that Helen had been engaged to marry Alex, but she had broken off the engagement after Helen had a dreadful accident that crippled her.

Cousin Helen left that evening, continuing on her way to a special clinic.

The next morning, Papa asked, 'What are you all going to do today?'

'Swing!' said John and Dorry both together. Aunt Izzie immediately said no, and told them not to use the swing until the next day. She did not tell them why.

In fact, the handyman, Alexander, had cracked one of the staples when putting up the swing, and had asked Aunt Izzie not to let anyone near it until it was safe.

Regardless, Katy went out and sat on the swing. She started moving to and fro, rising higher and higher steadily. Suddenly, there was a sharp crack. The swing spun half-around, and tossed Katy into the air.

The next thing Katy knew, Clover was kneeling beside her with a pale, scared face, and Aunt Izzie was dropping something cold and wet on her forehead. She slowly remembered what had happened.

When Katy tried to go upstairs, she could not. She fell back on the pillow and asked Aunt Izzy why she could not stand. Aunt Izzie said, 'I'm afraid you've sprained something.'

Dr Alsop arrived, examined Katy and said it only looked like a twist or a sprain. He instructed her to stay in bed for a few days.

One day, Katy suddenly became aware of the glaring light from the window that was usually shaded and wind blowing over her. She opened her eyes and saw Elsie fanning her.

'Don't be afraid,' said Elsie, 'I won't disturb you,' her little lips trembled. She insisted that the children would remain quiet and were sorry that she was sick.

Elsie pointed to the chair, which had a pewter tea-set, a box with a glass lid, a jointed doll, a transparent slate and two new lead pencils—gifts that Elsie and Johnnie had got for Katy.

Almost five weeks went by. Although the pain had almost gone, Katy still could not stand up by herself. Each day grew duller and duller, and she did not want to read or sew. She was too selfishly miserable to appreciate all the love and affection the others were showing her. Then, Cousin Helen sent her a note saying she would be returning home that week.

When Katy heard this she almost cried, and asked that Cousin Helen stop by on her way home. Papa agreed immediately, as did Aunt Izzie. Katy was so happy that she threw her arms round Aunt Izzie's neck for the first time in her life.

Cousin Helen reached at last. This time, Katy could not welcome her at the stairs, so Papa carried Cousin Helen upstairs and made her sit in a big chair beside Katy.

Almost sobbing, Katy asked, 'How do you manage to be so sweet, beautiful and patient when you're feeling bad all the time, and cannot do anything about it?'

Cousin Helen then asked if Katy's Papa thought she would get well eventually. Katy replied that he did, but that it would take time for her to recover.

Katy wanted to do so many things! She wanted to study, become famous and teach the children. And now, she could not go to school and learn and she feared that by the time she recovered, the children would be older and would not need her anymore.

Her cousin smiled, and said that God would take Katy to His school, where people learnt many beautiful things, just by lying in bed.

'It's called the School of Pain,' she said.

Cousin Helen added that the lessons would happen in Katy's own room. The rules were tough, even the lessons were not simple, but Cousin Helen insisted that the more she studied, the more interesting things would become.

'What are the lessons?' asked Katy.

Cousin Helen began by talking about one of the hardest lessons—patience. Then there were the lessons of cheerfulness and of making the best of things.

Katy then said, 'Sometimes there's nothing to make the best of.'

'Yes, there always is,' said Helen. She told Katy that everything in the world has two handles—the smooth handle, which held things lightly and easily, and the rough handle, which is hard to lift, and can hurt your hand.

Cousin Helen said there were other lessons. She spoke of the lesson of hopefulness, which had many teachers.

'The Sun is one such teacher,' she said. 'He sits outside the window all day waiting for a chance to slip in and get at his pupil. He's a first-rate teacher, too. I wouldn't shut him out, if I were you'.

'There is one more lesson, the lesson of neatness,' said Cousin Helen. 'School-rooms must be kept in order, you know. A sick person ought to be as fresh and dainty as a rose,' she added.

Katy decided she simply could not be neat and orderly like Cousin Helen, who Katy thought was born neat.

So Cousin Helen told her a story about a girl she knew, who was not born neat. This girl wanted to run, climb, ride and be active just like them, but an accident caused her to lie on her back for the rest of her life. Her situation was similar to Cousin Helen's, but not Katy's, since Katy would get well soon.

Cousin Helen said, 'Make the children feel that your room is the place to come to when they are tired, or happy, or grieved, or sorry about anything. The best time to help people is right now, when you are not busy with your own life.'

Just then, their Papa came in to take Cousin Helen back home. Katy held back her tears, remembering the lesson of patience.

As she was leaving, Cousin Helen told Katy, 'In this school, to which we belong, there is one

great comfort: our Teacher is always at hand, and ready to be there for us.'

Soon, two months passed. Katy strove to be better, and Cousin Helen sent her comforting gifts nearly every week.

Christmas was approaching, and Katy asked Aunt Izzie to let the children hang their stockings in her room. Katy wished she had gifts to give all the children. She found a sash to give Clover, and she had two dollars, but it was not nearly enough. Hearing this, Aunt Izzie produced a five-dollar note, which she had been planning to give Katy. Overjoyed, Katy asked Aunt Izzie to buy a writing desk for Elsie, a sled for Johnnie, books for Dorry and Cecy and a thimble for Mary, the nurse. How Aunt Izzie managed to buy so much with seven dollars we shall never know! Katy even asked Papa to buy Aunt Izzie a book she liked.

After supper, the children came up to hang their stockings and read out their wish lists for Santa Claus. After reading, they each tossed the piece of paper into the fire. Then, Aunt Izzie sent them all off to bed.

Katy felt bad that no one had offered to hang up a stocking for her, but she swept aside the thought. The next morning she was woken by the children in her nursery, all happy and excited with their presents. Katy found a beautiful little evergreen tree by her bed—decorated and hung with presents! The children had prepared it just for her. And the tree was perched on a chair which leaned back, a gift for Katy from her father.

It was several weeks before Katy was well enough to use the chair, but once she could, she would sit by the window and look outside. She grew more cheerful and before Valentine's Day, she and Cecy made a plan.

The day before Valentine's, each of the children received a special invitation for tea at 'Queen Katharine's Palace' at six o' clock.

That evening the children went up to Katy's brightly lit room. It was all set for a tea party. There was a cake, with the words 'St Valentine' iced on it. After they had all eaten, there was a knock on the door. Bridget, the maid, came in with an envelope for Clover. Clover opened it and found a green pincushion in the shape of a clover, and a note with a small poem about her! It was the first Valentine she had ever received, and she was enchanted by it.

There was another knock on the door. This time, Bridget brought a letter for Elsie. After this was read out, there was another knock, and a handful of letters were delivered, one for everyone. To Katy's surprise, there were two letters for her, including one from Cousin Helen.

Katy read Cousin Helen's letter after everyone fell asleep. It spoke about the schools that her cousin had mentioned, and how to approach her teachers.

Katy was keenly looking forward to spring. She wanted something to happen, and something did; but it was not a nice something.

Aunt Izzie fell ill with typhoid. The doctors said the house had to be quiet, so she could rest. So John, Dorry and Phil were sent to stay at Mrs Hall's house. Elsie and Clover promised to be good, so their Papa let them stay.

The children started to get worried, but little people tend to think that grown-ups are so strong and so big, that nothing can possibly happen to them. None of the children even thought that Aunt Izzie might not get better. So, it was a complete shock to Katy when Aunt Izzie passed away one night.

The three girls began crying in each other's arms, realizing how good their aunt had been to them. Katy cried herself to sleep that night, wondering what she would do without her.

A few days later, Papa came to Katy's room. He told Katy that they would be getting someone to do the housekeeping, and asked if she could manage for a few days until the new housekeeper arrived.

Katy insisted that her Papa allow her to try housekeeping. He wondered how she would manage, but Katy was very keen and sought the help of Clover and old Mary. Eventually, Papa agreed to let her try her hand at it for a month.

Katy's Papa had thought she would soon get bored with the idea, but he was mistaken. Housekeeping was not very hard work for Katy, since the maids knew Aunt Izzie's ways very well. As months passed, she learned to manage the house better. Papa watched her become brighter and brighter and felt that the experiment was a success.

Two years passed.

It was June, and Clover—now fourteen years old—had been practising on the piano. Elsie appeared and began chatting with Clover.

Just then, they heard a bell and ran upstairs to see what Katy wanted. Katy had been overseeing the maids, who were cleaning out Papa's room, and she met the girls at the door. She still could not walk, but cheerfully rolled around the house in a wheelchair.

She greeted them with a smile and said she had meant to only call Clover, since she feared Bridget would mess with their Papa's table. As she was heading there, she also asked her to get a pincushion. Katy had also asked Elsie to kindly fetch a drawer out of a table from their father's room.

By the time Clover returned, Dorry joined them. He had grown much wiser and, having a knack for mechanics, had fixed Katy's clock.

Dorry stayed there to make sure it was working properly. When the hour hand of the clock touched twelve, it began to strike. It kept going and going, and only stopped after striking half past one.

The girls found it hilarious, but Dorry was mortified. He asked Katy if he could take it away and fix it again. Clover told her not to, but Katy kindly gave it to Dorry suggesting that maybe someone in the clock repair shop could help him fix it.

Moments later, old Mary came in and asked Katy to speak to Alexander about putting the woodshed in order. Katy said that she would do so and ensure it was done well. After some time, there was another knock and, to their surprise, Imogen Clark entered.

She was visiting them after almost two years, only to say goodbye. Her family was moving to Jacksonville. Imogen chatted with Katy and Elsie for half an hour and left.

The children settled down to do their work, when the doorbell rang. Bridget came upstairs, looking disturbed and told Katy that Mrs Worrett had come to spend the day.

Aunt Izzie's old friend, Mrs Worrett lived about six miles away, and sometimes came to the Carr's for lunch, when she was out on work.

She asked if she should send Mrs Worrett away.

'Should I tell her you're busy, and can't see her?' Bridget asked. 'There's no proper lunch or anything today, you know.'

The Katy of two years ago may have jumped at this idea, but the Katy of today was more considerate.

'No, don't do that. We'll make the best of what we have,' she said.

Katy then asked Clover to run down and tell Mrs Worrett that the dining room was in confusion and they would have lunch in her room, once the old woman had rested and freshened up.

'I can't bear to send the poor old lady away when she has come so far,' Katy told Elsie when the others had left, and warned her not to giggle at Mrs Worrett.

Elsie always giggled at Mrs Worrett, who was the most enormously fat person they had ever seen. She looked like she weighed a 1,000 pounds.

The maids brought up their lunch and Mrs Worrett ate a lot. She seemed to enjoy everything, and would not get up until four o' clock. The girls felt like the afternoon would never end; they had to struggle to think of what to say to their vast guest. Finally, as she was getting ready to leave, Mrs Worrett thanked Katy for treating her so well, and said that Aunt Izzie would have been proud of her. Katy was extremely satisfied to hear this.

Almost six weeks after Mrs Worrett's visit, Clover and Elsie were busy with their work when they were startled by the sound of Kate's bell ringing agitatedly.

They both ran up to see Katy in her chair, looking extremely excited.

'I stood up,' she said.

The others were too astonished to say anything.

Katy said, 'Suddenly, I had the feeling that if I tried I could, so I did try, and there I was, up and out of the chair; but I held onto the chair all the time! I was so frightened.'

Clover rushed downstairs to inform the rest of them, but their Papa was out. When Papa came back, he was as excited as them. He started questioning Katy, making her stand up and sit down. It was the first time that the children had seen Papa so excited.

As Papa predicted, Katy's progress was slow. At first, she could not stand for more than a minute, which then reached five minutes, holding the chair tightly all the while. After this, she started walking one step at a time, with a chair before her. At the same time, Clover and Elsie would move around her anxiously.

By the end of August, Katy insisted that she could walk up and down the stairs, but Papa told her she had to wait. He said she must only walk down after ten days, which happened to fall on the day before their Mamma's birthday. She then decided to walk down on the eighth of September, her mother's birthday.

Katy then sat and looked out of the

window in a particularly happy mood. She wondered if she was really going to say goodbye to Pain. She could now see 'Love in the Pain' and wondered how good the Teacher had been to her.

It was now one day before the momentous occasion. Katy was going to wear a brand new dress the day she walked down the stairs. As she sat down to read her book, she heard a noise, like people giggling and walking on the stairs.

The next day, the children were all wearing their best clothes. Papa told Katy to rest as soon as she reached the bottom step. Katy leaned on Papa, with Dorry on the side and the other girls behind her.

Papa opened the parlour door. Katy took one step at a time, and suddenly stopped. To her surprise, Cousin Helen was sitting on the sofa. Forgetting her weakness, Katy held out her arms and ran to Helen. She stumbled along the way, but managed to reach her cousin and hug her. Cousin Helen was delighted to see Katy recovered.

The house was filled with joy, laughter and happiness. Helen told Katy that her hard work and bravery had helped her. Katy thought she didn't deserve it, but I think she did.

Rebecca
of Sunnybrook Farm

Kate Douglas Wiggin

FRESH
PAINT

Mr Jeremiah Cobb was stepping out of the Maplewood post office when a woman asked him if he was going to Riverboro and could he take a girl in his carriage with him to that town. Mr Cobb said 'Yes' and a child, standing there with a bouquet of lilacs and a bundle, was helped by the woman into the carriage.

'I want you to take her to my sisters Mirandy and Jane Sawyer's brick house there. Do you know them?'

Mr Cobb said he did.

'They are waiting for Rebecca. Please take good care of her.' The woman then said goodbye to Rebecca and told her not to trouble Mr Cobb.

'I won't,' Rebecca said.

The girl wanted a front seat with Mr Cobb and he helped her get it. Mr Cobb looked closely at the girl and admired her beautiful eyes. All through the trip, Rebecca spoke about herself, her brothers and sisters, her parents and their Sunnybrook Farm.

Rebecca also expressed a desire to visit Milltown and Mr Cobb said he would take her there if her aunt permitted it. As they approached their destination, Rebecca said she would like to get into the carriage again and Mr Cobb helped her return to her seat.

Mr Cobb escorted Rebecca like she was a lady when they stopped at the house and the girl gave the bunch of flowers to her Aunt Miranda who kissed her with little interest on her cheek.

Mirandy told Rebecca that her room was upstairs. She added, 'Close the door with the mosquito netting behind you and do things the correct way. Use the back stairs always. When you're ready, come down.'

Rebecca shut the door without saying a word.

That night Mr Cobb told all these things to his wife.

Every day, Rebecca walked to the school at the Riverboro Centre, and soon made friends with Emma Jane Perkins.

Often, the girls took a shortcut to school and sometimes bumped into the Simpson children in their old, repaired clothes. They reminded Rebecca of her family at Sunnybrook Farm.

Rebecca had a busy and entertaining first summer in Riverboro with her books and new friends. But, in her letter to her mother, she said she did not like Aunt Miranda as much as she did Aunt Jane.

Rebecca just could not like Mirandy, who wanted Rebecca to be an angel when Rebecca only wanted to be a good person. Consequently, she frequently annoyed her aunt. Worse, Rebecca reminded Miranda of her father, Lorenzo de Medici Randall, who Miranda disliked intensely. She thought LDM Randall had been a foolish and worthless man, who deceived her sister, Aurelia (Rebecca's mother) with his good manners and handsome face.

Aunt Miranda liked Hannah, Rebecca's older sister, better. But Aunt Jane treated Rebecca well and made quick excuses as the child tried to adjust to her new life in the 'brick house.'

One afternoon Minnie Smellie, one of Rebecca's classmates, yelled 'Jailbird!' at the Simpson children. This was because Mr Simpson often landed in jail due to some crime. A furious Rebecca told Minnie that she would slap her if she taunted the Simpsons again. After that a scared Minnie kept quiet whenever she met the Simpsons.

On Friday, at a school recitation, Rebecca drew the USA flag on the blackboard and also a drawing of Columbia, which everyone liked especially her teacher, Miss Dearborn.

Rebecca, who had never been praised even once in her life, was so thrilled that she could not remember her dialogue. When the children were sent home to change their clothes, Rebecca, who put on her pink dress and held her pink umbrella, looked 'as pretty beautiful as a picture!' as Emma Jane put it.

Though every student put on a good performance, Rebecca was the star of the show. But she was brought down to earth when she returned home.

Aunt Miranda was waiting for her at the doorway.

'Dancing just like her father, and flaunting her new dress and umbrella,' she said to Jane. 'Rebecca, why did you wear your new dress without my permission? You could have ruined it in the rain.'

It had started raining just after Rebecca reached home.

'You were not at home so I could not ask you,' replied Rebecca.

'And you did not close the netting or put away the lunch dishes. You also kept the side door open!'

Rebecca got a solid scolding. She started to cry as she attempted to clarify the mistakes she had made.

Aunt Miranda told her, 'You are causing problems in the house…all airs and dressing up like your worthless father!'

Rebecca retorted, 'Aunt, I'll be good and obedient. But don't speak badly about my father. He was a lovely father.'

Rebecca went to her bedroom with a heavy heart. She had made up her mind. She would go back to the farm. Of course, her mother would be upset but Hannah could take her place at Riverboro. She packed her toothbrush, night dress and comb in a bundle and gently dropped it to the ground outside and quickly followed the bundle, using the lightning rod as a guide. Soon, she was on her way on that stormy evening.

Jeremiah Cobb was having dinner, when he looked up and suddenly saw Rebecca's teary face through the window.

'My lady passenger! Have you come to spend an evening with Uncle Jerry?' he asked.

Rebecca started crying again and told Mr Cobb that she had run away. She asked if he would help her return to Sunnybrooke.

When Mr Cobb said he would take care of her, she said, 'Mother won't be happy but I'll explain things to her.'

As they discussed fresh ideas, Mr Cobb tried to think of ways to convince Rebecca to stay.

'Miss Dearborn thinks you are a terrific student and if she had more like you she'd teach all the time!' he said.

Rebecca's face sparkled when she heard this.

Mr Cobb went on, 'You have a good opportunity here. Miranda gives you a home, clothes and schooling, and plans to send you to the expensive school, Wareham. I agree that she is unpleasant and you are not very patient, so it can be tough to live with her. But she is helping you and you must repay her with good behaviour. Will you give it up just because of your aunt?'

Rebecca sat thinking for a while.

Soon, it stopped raining and a rainbow appeared in the sky. Mr Cobb asked her, 'When shall we leave for Sunnybrook?'

Rebecca stood up and said quietly, 'We won't go back. I'll stay here and behave nicely.'

Mr Cobb was overjoyed.

'Now here's my plan. I'll take you to the house; you slip in by the side door. I'll get Miranda and Jane the wood they had asked for. When they go to the shed, you run upstairs to your bedroom,' he said.

Rebecca's anger at Aunt Miranda had disappeared. She decided to win her over and to forget the horrible remarks Aunt Miranda had made about her father.

Miranda noticed the change in the little girl.

'The scolding did her good,' she told Jane on Saturday.

'I'm happy for you,' Jane replied. 'Now, allow me to take Rebecca and Emma Jane to the riverside tomorrow afternoon and invite Emma Jane for supper on Sunday. Then allow her go to Milltown with Mr and Mrs Cobbs on Wednesday.'

Milltown was just like Rebecca thought it would be—though not as nice as Venice and Rome, which Rebecca had read about.

Mrs Cobb was pleased with Rebecca's company that Wednesday.

'Did you see her in the tent where Uncle Tom's Cabin was being enacted? Harriet Beecher Stowe herself could not have done it better!' she told Mr Cobb.

'I observed everything,' replied Mr Cobb, and added that he was pleased 'Mother' shared his opinion of Rebecca. The couple decided the girl would grow up to become a great writer or poet.

But Rebecca's writing did not satisfy Miss Dearborn.

'Write as you talk, Rebecca,' said poor Miss Dearborn.

'Miss Dearborn! If I don't have anything to say, I can't write, can I?'

'Compositions are like that,' Miss Dearborn replied doubtfully. 'You have to say something. On "solitude", you did not say anything interesting. You used too many "yours" and "yous" in it. You must say "one"—like "One does not read a good book often."—and that too very infrequently.'

Rebecca rewrote her essay on 'solitude', in accordance with Miss Dearborn's advice, but neither teacher nor student was pleased with the effort.

Rebecca, was out with the Cobbs, when she leant over a rail to better enjoy the view of the water flowing under the bridge. She was lost as she mentally composed a poem, until she smelled fresh paint and realized she was wearing her best dress.

'Paint!' she cried, 'On my best dress! What will Aunt Miranda say?'

Mrs Cobb promised to remove the stains, and cleaned the dress partially with turpentine. It looked slightly better and Rebecca felt relieved. She left it to dry and noted down the poem she had composed on the bridge. The Cobbs thought it was marvellous and asked for a copy to keep.

But the pattern of the dress was spoilt, the colours faded and muddy streaks were seen. They smoothed it with a hot iron, and Rebecca wore it.

The dirty spots were visible but Rebecca said, 'If I have to get a scolding, I want to get it quickly done!'

Rebecca took the scolding bravely. Aunt Miranda said that an absent-minded girl would surely grow up to be a worthless person! She banned Rebecca from attending Alice Robinson's birthday party and told her she would have to wear the ruined dress until it was worn out. After six months, Aunt Jane added a frilled apron neatly shaped to conceal the spots on the dress.

As Thanksgiving approached, the Simpsons were in crisis. They did not have much to eat and very little to wear. The children depended on charity to feed themselves; not everyone liked them, but some kind souls did give them leftovers.

In chilly November, as sumptuous meals were being cooked in other people's houses, the poor Simpsons had to be satisfied selling soap. They sold enough soap in autumn to get a small handcart, which they planned to use to expand their business to nearby villages.

The soap factory gave very little cash to new agents, but promised them gifts or incentives. The Simpsons would be eligible for three incentives—a bookcase, a luxurious reclining chair and a festive lamp—if they sold a higher number of soaps. They dreamt of the lamp, which they desired more than food, clothing or drink. So Rebecca joined in the effort to sell soap for the Simpsons.

Soon, Emma Jane Perkins also joined the team, which met at the Perkins' attic to formulate a sales plan. They used the soap company's information to prepare their sales plan, helped by sections of a discourse that a patent-medicine seller had given at the Milltown Fair.

The children worked singly, and Emma Jane had sold three single cakes while Rebecca had three boxes. In one house, Rebecca entered by the side door, and met a young, good-looking man in a rocking-chair.

He seemed to be from the city and a shy Rebecca asked for the lady of the house.

'Presently, I am that lady,' the stranger said smilingly. 'Can I do anything for you?'

'Do you require soap?' Rebecca asked.

'Do you feel I require soap?' he replied.

A smiling Rebecca said, 'I did not mean THAT. I am selling soaps. I want to show you a remarkable soap. It's the finest in the market...'

'Oh! Tell more about that soap,' the gentleman said kindly.

Rebecca's smiles grew and her new friend invited her to sit on a stool by him. The girl told him all about the soaps—the Rose-Red and the Snow-White—and their prices.

When she asked if he lived alone, the pleasant gentleman explained that he did not live there.

'I'm only visiting my aunt,' he said, 'she's away in Portland. I used to live here when I was a boy. I like this place very much.'

Rebecca said, 'I don't feel anything can take the place of the house where one stayed when one was young,'—and almost burst with pleasure for having successfully made correct use of the indefinite pronoun 'one' in a conversation!

'My past was quite unpleasant,' the stranger said.

'Mine was too,' said Rebecca. She asked him what his worst troubles were.

'Little food and few clothes.'

Rebecca said in sympathy, 'Oh! Mine were no shoes, too few books and too many babies! Now you're happy and all right, aren't you?' she asked him with some doubts because when not speaking, his face had a cheerless look.

'I'm doing quite well,' the man replied, smiling delightfully.

'Tell me—how many soaps must I purchase today?'

'How many would your aunt need?'

'What will you do with the large profits from selling these soaps?'

Rebecca said confidentially, 'We are selling these for someone else. I live with my aunts. My friend there at the gate is the daughter of a wealthy blacksmith. She doesn't require money. We are attempting to earn a premium for our friends.'

Rebecca then unexpectedly started describing the plight of the Simpson family—their unhappy life and poverty and their need of a festive lamp to lighten up their life.

When Rebecca told him about the soap company's incentive scheme, the young man said, 'Well, I'll buy 300 cakes of soap. That should get them any gift they want.'

A surprised Rebecca tried suddenly to run away. The young man caught her and told her to never be surprised when given a big order.

He then asked, 'What's your name?'

'Rebecca Rowena Randall.'

'Do you know what my name is?'

'I know,' Rebecca answered brightly. 'You have to be Mr Aladdin! Can I now run and tell Emma Jane? She will be tired of waiting for me!'

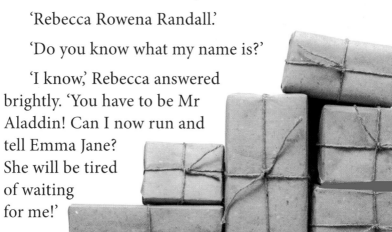

Rebecca raced away shouting, 'Emma Jane! We have sold all!'

Mr Aladdin came after her. He carried all the soap boxes from the wagon, took the circular and said he would write to the soap company regarding the incentive.

'It would be a pleasant surprise if the lamp arrived at the Simpsons' on Thanksgiving,' he said, and asked Rebecca and Emma Jane to keep this a secret.

The girls happily agreed and thanked him.

'I was a kind of salesman many years ago and I like it when things are well done. Goodbye, Miss Rowena!'

'Bye, Mr Aladdin!' Rebecca said and delightfully waved her hand at Mr Aladdin.

The girls, with great effort, kept their astonishing news a secret. When Thanksgiving came, the lamp also arrived in a big box. Rebecca waited till it was nearly dark and then asked if she could visit the Simpsons.

'Why, on Thanksgiving Day?' asked Aunt Miranda.

'They have got a new lamp, and Emma Jane and I promised them we would go to see it all lit up, and celebrate with a party.'

'The children won the lamp as a reward for selling soaps,' Rebecca explained. 'Emma Jane and I helped them.'

Aunt Miranda then gave her permission to go, but for one hour only.

The Burnham sisters, who were guests for Thanksgiving dinner, noted that they had never seen a child improve as quickly as Rebecca.

'I didn't think the children would be able to sell anything,' Miranda said.

Miss Ellen Burnham said, 'Adam Ladd said the girl who sold the soaps at the Ladds' house in North Riverboro was a very remarkable child.'

'I would never call Clara Belle remarkable,' said Miss Miranda.

'Adam's aunt says he would send a Christmas gift to the girl who sold the soaps,' Miss Ellen said.

Miss Miranda said, 'Clara Belle has red hair and her eye is not good. However, the more Adam gives her, the less the town's people will have to.'

'Is there any other Simpson girl?' Miss Lydia Burnham asked. 'Adam said this girl had very beautiful eyes and that's what made him purchase three hundred cakes.'

Aunt Jane thought, 'What Riverboro child was winning and remarkable except for Rebecca? Who had beautiful eyes—except Rebecca? And which child could persuade a man to buy 300 cakes of soap—except Rebecca?'

'They had an actual Thanksgiving dinner,' Emma Jane told Rebecca when they met on the way to the Simpsons. Father sent them a spare rib; the doctor, sweet potatoes, turnips and cranberries; and Mrs Cobb, mince-meat and a chicken.'

The lamp was the main attraction at the party. Just its presence was entertaining.

'Rebecca, who sold the soap to Mr Ladd in North Riverboro?' Miss Jane asked when Rebecca went home.

'Mr who?' asked Rebecca.

'Mr Ladd. Adam Ladd.'

Rebecca laughed to herself when she realized her Mr Aladdin was actually called Adam Ladd.

'Emma Jane and I,' she replied.

As winter arrived, Rebecca attempted to be careful with her chores and quiet while playing. Then, they received news that Rebecca's beloved brother John had gone to be with Cousin Ann, whose husband had passed away. John would get an education in return for taking care of the cow, horse and barn. Cousin Ann's husband had been a doctor, and John would now get to study the old doctor's medical books. John had always wanted to become a doctor.

In December, Rebecca spent weeks making Christmas presents for her family. She designed a decorative tea-cosy with 'M' embroidered on it for Aunt Miranda, and a beautiful frilled pincushion with a 'J' on it for Aunt Jane.

Soon, Christmas Day dawned clear and fresh. Rebecca excitedly opened her presents—a grey muffler from Aunt Miranda, a green cashmere dress from Aunt Jane, a lovely 'tatting' collar from her mother, red mittens from Mrs Cobb and a handkerchief from Emma Jane.

During breakfast, a boy delivered a parcel for Rebecca.

There were two gifts inside. Rebecca nervously opened the small parcel addressed to her. Inside, was a long chain of beautiful pink coral beads, which ended in a cross of coral rosebuds. Underneath, was a card that said, 'Merry Christmas from Mr Aladdin'.

The other package was a silver chain with a blue enamel locket, for Emma Jane. An accompanying letter was addressed to 'Dear Miss Rebecca Rowena'.

In the letter, Mr Ladd said his aunt was delighted with the soaps, and that he would visit Rebecca that afternoon on his new sleigh. When he came, Mr Ladd met Rebecca's aunts while she sat quietly on a stool near the fireplace.

That evening, Rebecca thought back about the day and was very happy. A sleigh ride, happiness, lots of talking, excitement, the green dress, the touch of pink in the necklace—it had been a glorious Christmas Day.

A few days later, Mr Simpson returned home, and the whole family left town with everything they owned. Along the way, Mr Simpson managed to exchange the lamp for an old bicycle. The children were heartbroken. When he found that he could not console the children over the loss of the lamp, Mr Simpson rode away on the bicycle and was never heard of again.

Next, news reached the brick house that Mira, Rebecca's sister, had died. Rebecca returned home for two weeks. With Mira's death and John's absence, it was a sad homecoming. Hannah had now grown into a woman. Rebecca felt sorry for her sister, and wanted to give Hannah the chance to get away from the hard work on the farm. She suggested that Hannah go to the brick house, while she stayed back at Sunnybrook. But Hannah refused, saying she had plenty to do at the farm, she hated school and she would have lots of friends after New Year.

Soon, Rebecca finished school and was studying at Wareham.

One Wednesday, aunts Jane and Miranda were both ill, so Rebecca had to represent the family at the

Aid Society meeting to meet Reverend Amos Burch and his wife, missionaries who had just returned from Syria.

The service, held in the Sunday school room, started with a prayer. Rebecca played the melodeon with ease. She was enthralled to be introduced to an entirely new world.

'If we could be provided space,' Mr Burch said, he and his wife would stay there that night and the next day. 'Then we can organize a parlour meeting, where we can show you some specimens of Syrian handiwork, and tell you more about our educational methods.'

When no one else did, Rebecca invited the Burches to stay at the brick house on behalf of her aunts. They then asked her to close the prayer, which she did, timidly. Mr Burch said she must now become a member of the church.

Aunt Miranda was not pleased with Rebecca's actions.

'Why did you invite them?' she ask.

'I thought you would like their interesting company,' Rebecca said.

Rebecca added that Mrs Robinson had told her at the meeting that her grandparents always invited the missionaries when they visited. Then, she said she would get the guests' rooms ready and ran upstairs.

The missionaries came on time with their two children. Jane escorted them upstairs and Miranda supervized the cooking.

Later, Jane helped to put the food away, and Miranda entertained everyone in the parlour. Rebecca washed the dishes with the children helping her.

Since her aunts were unwell, Rebecca got up very early the next morning. She found that Miss Jane's health had deteriorated overnight, and she could not get up from her bed that morning. Miss Jane wondered how Miranda would manage without her.

However, the day passed smoothly, and the Burches left in the evening.

The missionaries' visit marked a turning point at the brick house. Soon, it was Miranda herself who kept the house ready for guests. Rebecca's life too changed, and she decided to complete the four years' course at Wareham, in three.

Emma Jane had gone to Edgewood High School for one week, but joined Wareham because Rebecca was there. She was not a very good student, but Emma Jane studied hard.

Among the teachers at Wareham who influenced Rebecca greatly was Miss Emily

Maxwell who taught her English literature and composition.

One day, somebody looked in, somebody who said, 'Miss Maxwell told me I should find Miss Rebecca Randall here.'

The voice startled Rebecca. She looked up and joyfully said, 'Mr Aladdin! Oh! I knew you were in Wareham, and I was afraid you wouldn't have time to come and see us.'

'Who is "us"? Oh, you mean the rich blacksmith's daughter?'

'Yes, she's my roommate,' answered Rebecca.

'Well, little Miss Rebecca,' he said, 'Whenever I go to Portland for a meeting with the railway directors there, I visit the school and give my advice.'

'I can't think of you as the school trustee,' said Rebecca.

He answered, 'I accepted the trusteeship in memory of my mother, whose last happy years were spent here.'

'Would you like to see my mother, Miss Rebecca?' Mr Ladd asked, holding out a slim leather case.

Rebecca took the case gently and opened it to find a picture of an innocent-looking girl. 'Oh, what a sweet face!' she whispered softly.

'She suffered many hardships,' said Adam. 'There was no one to protect her. Now I have success and money and power. But all that has come to me seems useless, since I cannot share it with her!'

Rebecca said, 'I'm so glad I could see her when she was young and happy. Perhaps, she is happy to see you now from heaven.'

'You are very kind, Rebecca,' said Adam, rising from his chair.

'Goodbye!' he said, taking her slim brown hands in his hands.

Rebecca did well in her first year at Wareham. In the second year, she was elected assistant editor of the Wareham School newspaper, *The Pilot*. But she was

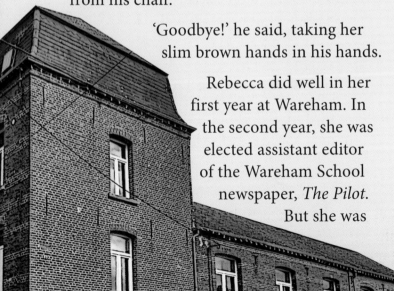

anxious and fearful at home. Aunt Miranda did not stop finding fault with her and this upset Rebecca very much. One Saturday, she cried with Aunt Jane because of this.

'You must be patient,' she said, 'because Aunt Miranda is not well and she has other problems also.'

All the temper faded from Rebecca's face, and she stopped crying and said, 'Oh! The poor dear thing! I won't mind a bit what she says now.'

Things were not good at Sunnybrook Farm either: the crops had failed and Aurelia was sick, among other things. The only good news was Hannah's engagement to Will Melville—a young farmer.

When Adam Ladd had met Mr Morrison of Wareham, he had said he wished the boys and girls of the two upper classes to compete in an essay writing competition. The two best essays would win fifty dollars!

Then, Mr Ladd met with Miss Maxwell. He told her how he had first met Rebecca and the two of them decided to ensure the girl's welfare.

The essay competition was very much on Rebecca's mind. She did not think she could be happy unless she won it; but that was only because she wanted to please Mr Aladdin and justify his belief in her.

For a long time, Rebecca could not decide what to write about. Finally, she wrote a story about a poor princess who was very grateful for all the help she had received.

The prize was to be announced after the term ended. Rebecca's entry won, and she used the money to pay off the mortgage on Sunnybrook Farm. The Governor, who read her story, praised Rebecca for it.

A year later, it was Rebecca's turn to graduate. Emma Jane was not graduating with Rebecca.

Rebecca saw Hannah and her husband in the audience, dear old John and cousin Ann. She felt a pang at the absence of her mother, who would not be coming. The Cobbs were there too. But Aunt Jane was not present.

It was over! The diplomas had been presented, and each girl had gone forward to receive the roll of degree with a bow. Rounds of applause greeted each graduate at this thrilling moment!

After the crowd had thinned a little, Adam Ladd went to the platform.

Rebecca turned from speaking to some strangers and met him in the aisle.

'Oh, Mr Aladdin, I am so glad you could come! Tell me, Mr Aladdin, are you happy?' Rebecca asked.

'More than happy!' he said.

Rebecca's heart was beating fast on hearing his praises, but before she could thank him, the Cobbses—Aunt Sarah and Uncle Jerry—arrived, and she introduced them to Mr Ladd.

'Where is Aunt Jane?' she asked, holding Aunt Sarah's and Uncle Jerry's hands.

'I'm sorry, dear, but we've got bad news for you.'

'Is Aunt Miranda worse?' and the colour in Rebecca's face faded.

'She had a second stroke yesterday morning… Jane said you should not know anything about it until the graduation ceremony was over.'

'I will go right home with you, Aunt Sarah.'

'Miranda's got her speech back, your aunt has just sent a letter saying she's better; and I'm going to stay with you tonight so you can have a good sleep. Pack your things tomorrow.'

Meanwhile, Adam Ladd had been talking with Mr Cobb. Mr Cobb was trying to find out what

Mr Ladd thought about Rebecca. He was happy to learn that Adam was fond of Rebecca.

'I believe, though, that happier days are coming for her,' Adam Ladd said. 'It is a secret now, but the new railroad will buy Mrs Randall's farm. The station will be built on the farm. She will receive 6,000 dollars which will give her an income of 300 or 400 dollars a year, if she will allow me to invest it for her.'

Rebecca did not see her aunt Miranda until she had been at the brick house for several days. Miranda steadfastly refused to have anyone but Jane in the room until her face had regained its natural look.

Then came a morning when she asked for Rebecca. The door was opened and Rebecca stood there, her hands full of sweet peas. After a long pause Rebecca sat down by the bedside and told her how much she loved her.

Finally, the day came when Rebecca had to leave and start a new life. Then, when all was ready, came a telegram from Hannah, 'Come at once. Mother has had a bad accident.'

In less than an hour Rebecca started on her way to Sunnybrook. Her mother had fractured her right knee and hurt her back, but was conscious and in no immediate danger.

Meanwhile, back at the brick house, Miranda decided to give the brick house to Rebecca in her will, and permitted Jane to get Aurelia and her children to the old brick house.

One day, Hannah's husband, Will, tossed a letter into Rebecca's lap.

'Sister is keeping well,' said Aurelia gratefully, 'or Jane would have telegraphed. See what she says.'

The brief letter said, 'Aunt Miranda passed away an hour back. I will not have the funeral until you come here. She died suddenly and was not in any pain. —Aunt Jane.'

Mr Cobb's carriage arrived and Rebecca was on her way home. As Rebecca entered the gate, the house door opened. Aunt Jane walked down the steps, sad and weak. Rebecca held out her arms.

It was again her home now. It was the shelter for the small family at Sunnybrook. Her mother again would have the companionship of her sister and her girlhood friends. The children would have playmates and teachers.

People often regarded ten-year-old Mary Lennox as quite a disagreeable child. It was not untrue; Mary, who was born in India, had a thin little face and a thin body. Her hair and her skin were yellow because she was often ill. Little Mary's father was a busy man who held a position with the British government and her mother—Mrs Lennox, while very beautiful—was more interested in merrymaking and sought to amuse herself with the people around her. Mary was often neglected, and often entirely in the care of an Indian nanny. Mary grew into a selfish young girl; she cared for no one and showed nobody any kindness.

One morning when Mary awoke, she found there was a new maid. Mary did not want anyone else to tend to her, so she threw a tantrum and ran outdoors to play in the garden.

There, Mary overheard her mother talking to someone. She heard that her nanny had died of cholera. An epidemic had broken out and had reached the Lennox household, too. The adults were all very worried and chaos reigned. Mary did not like the noise and confusion. So she hid in her room and refused to come out. When she came out the next day, the house was empty. Everyone she knew, including her parents, had either died or like the maids, had left.

Soon, a group of British soldiers came to the house, and took Mary to live with a British clergyman and his five children.

Mary and the children hated each other immediately. By the second day of her stay, the children, began to tease her using a rhyme.

'Mistress Mary, quite contrary,

How does your garden grow?

With silver bells, and cockle shells,

And marigolds all in a row.'

The little boy Basil started it and the other children soon joined in, dancing around her singing, laughing and annoying her. Mary was furious.

Later, Basil told Mary that, by the end of the week, she would be sent back to England to live with her uncle, Archibald Craven. The only problem was that Mary had never met or even heard of this uncle.

Two days later, she set sail for England, and met Mrs Medlock, her uncle's housekeeper, whom Mary considered one of the most disagreeable women she had ever met.

On the train journey from London to Yorkshire, Mrs Medlock told Mary tales about Mr Craven, who was a hunchback and a widower. According to the housekeeper, Mrs Craven's death had been the end of her uncle's hope and

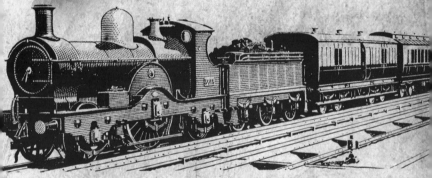

happiness. Since her aunt died, he had kept most of the hundred rooms of his house locked.

After arriving at Yorkshire, Mrs Medlock and Mary took a carriage to Mr Craven's house at Misselthwaite Manor. On reaching the huge mansion, Mrs Medlock showed Mary her room, and instructed her to confine herself to her room and the one next to it.

Thus, Mary arrived at Misselthwaite Manor, where she felt more uncomfortable than she had felt in all her life.

Martha, one of Misselthwaite Manor's numerous maids, woke up Mary on her first morning there. Mary told Martha that she did not like the moor.

'That's only because you're not used to it,' Martha replied kindly. 'You will come to love it, just as I did.'

The next day, Mary was pleased to discover that all her black mourning clothes had been replaced by a new set of bright white woollen clothes.

To make Mary more comfortable, Martha told the little girl about her family: her parents and her eleven siblings.

'Our Dickon's got a young pony,' Martha said about her youngest brother. 'He's a kind lad and animals love him!'

Mary, who had never had a pet of any kind, was fascinated by the thought of Dickon. When Martha suggested Mary explore the moor, she agreed hoping that she might meet Dickon.

As weeks passed, Mary got into a routine. She would finish her breakfast and explore the moor and the manor's surroundings. She made a few friends too: an old gardener called Ben Weatherstaff and his friend, the robin.

In her conversations with Ben and Martha, Mary soon discovered the existence of a secret garden on the Misselthwaite grounds. It had

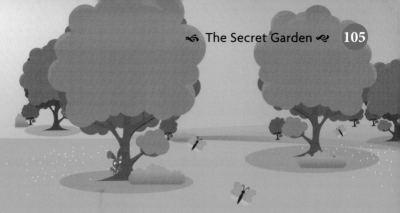

been kept locked for ten years. It used to be Mrs Craven's garden. However, after she died, Mr Craven had locked the gate and buried the key.

Mary's health gradually improved with her explorations and excursions into the moors.

One afternoon, while walking along the manor grounds, Mary saw Ben's robin again. She chased it as it flew along the walls of the garden, and into the secret garden. Mary was convinced that the robin lived in the secret garden.

That evening, when Mary told her about the robin and the garden, Martha said that Mr and Mrs Craven spent many cheerful afternoons in the garden. Mrs Craven had liked to sit on one of the high, rose-covered bowers. One day, the branch had given way and Mrs Craven had fallen to the ground. Her injuries did not heal, and she later died. After that day, Mr Craven locked the gate and forbade everyone from entering the garden.

When Mary heard this, she felt a great pity for her uncle.

During the conversation, Mary heard a strange noise through the whistling of the wind. It sounded like a child crying. It seemed to Mary to be coming from inside the house!

'Do you hear anyone crying?' she asked.

Martha looked confused.

'No,' she said. 'Sometimes the wind sounds like someone was lost on the moor and wailing.'

'Listen,' Mary said.

Just then, a door must have been opened somewhere downstairs for the light was blown out and the crying sound was swept down the far corridor so that it was heard clearer than ever.

Again, Martha insisted it was the wind, but Mary did not believe her.

The following day, a rainstorm confined Mary to the manor. Since she could not explore the moor, she decided to explore the mansion and its numerous locked rooms. At one point, she came across beautiful paintings of children. She was fascinated by one painting—it was of a young girl with a parrot perched on her finger.

'I wish you could keep me company,' she murmured to the little girl in the painting.

Suddenly, Mary heard the little child scream again. She set off in the direction from which the sound was coming. But she ran into Mrs Medlock, who had been searching for her. The older lady scolded her and sent her back to the room.

Once the rainstorm was over, Mary went out onto the moor again. Again, she saw the robin and followed it to a patch of freshly turned earth.

There, buried in the soil, was a tarnished old key—possibly it was the key to the secret garden.

Mary decided that if she could only find the door to the secret garden, she could spend hours in peaceful solitude, without anyone ever finding her.

The next day, Martha told Mary that she would soon be visiting her mother.

By now, Mary had heard so many stories about Martha's family. In fact, she had grown quite fond of Martha's mother and her brother Dickon.

'Could I visit your mother too?' she asked.

Martha said she would ask her mother and let her know. Martha's mother, Mrs Sowerby, said yes, as long as Mr Cravens said she could.

One afternoon, while Mary was walking along the ivy-covered walls of the manor, she bumped into Ben. He was in a good mood, tending to the plants.

'Can you smell that?' he asked Mary.

'I smell something damp and fresh and wet,' she replied sniffing the air.

'That's the spring time coming,' he remarked. 'It's always dull in winter. But soon, the sun will warm up the earth and little green spikes will shoot up from the ground.'

Using this as an opportunity Mary asked him about the secret garden and whether there was anything in there. He said that only his friend, the robin would know since no one had been in there since it had been locked up.

Mary then wandered off. She was thinking that, since she was born just around ten years ago, that garden had been shut almost all her life. She also realized that she was fond of the people around her—Martha, Dickon, their mother and even the robin, whom she considered more of a person than a bird—for the first time since she could remember.

A gust of wind disturbed some of the vines along the wall. Curious, Mary examined it closely and found a locked door beneath it.

Mary pulled out the key she had unearthed the day before and unlocked the door. She was now standing in the forbidden secret garden.

Mary was awestruck by her discovery. Looking around the garden she found rosebushes and more beautiful roses that, perhaps because of the lack of grooming, had reached the height of trees. Some of the vines and creepers looked like beautiful flowerless curtains in the air. Unfortunately, the cold winter snows had turned everything brown and grey. She hoped that something was still alive.

The garden soon became the centre of Mary's world. When she discovered a few green shoots emerging from the earth, she started weeding the whole place, eagerly hoping for a new life in the spring.

One night, Mary asked Martha about gardening tools. Martha suggested she write to Dickon. Mary was quite excited about the prospect of meeting him—the boy who was adored by animals. However, before Martha could leave the room, Mary heard the usual cry of a child in the distance. She asked Martha about it, but the older girl refused to admit that she had heard anyone crying and rushed out.

Mary continued spending most of her time tending to the plants, even though she did not know much about gardening.

One day, Dickon responded to her letter. He had with him the tools and seeds that she had requested. When Mary finally met Dickon, she found him to be a healthy-looking boy with patchwork clothes and a Yorkshire accent. She soon forgot her shyness and the two quickly became comfortable with each other.

'May I see the place where these seeds are to be sown?' Dickon asked politely, after handing her the equipment.

Mary hesitated. She was unsure of trusting anyone with the secret of the forbidden garden.

'You can trust me. I won't tell anyone,' Dickon said, 'I keep many secrets you know.'

Dickon insisted and, finally, she took him into her confidence.

'I have the key to a secret garden,' said Mary cautiously.

The two of them planned to rebuild the garden until Mary was called for supper.

Back at the manor, Martha told Mary that her uncle, Mr Craven, had returned from his trip. He had met Martha's mother, Susan Sowerby, in the village, and Mrs Sowerby had scolded him for neglecting his duties towards his niece.

Mr Craven responded that he needed to see Mary right away to ensure that she was being taken care of, Martha added, since he would be leaving Misselthwaite Manor again the following day.

Based on her past experiences, Mary was certain that she and her uncle would hate each other instantly. However, when she entered his chambers to meet him, she was surprised to find that he was not quite the hunchback people said he was, although his shoulders were slightly crooked.

He apologized for having neglected her and asked if she was being cared for.

'Would you like a governess?' he then asked.

'I would rather just play on the moor,' Mary said, 'I'm too big for a nurse.'

'Where do you play?' he asked, kindly.

'Everywhere,' said Mary. 'Martha's mother sent me a skipping rope. I skip and run; and I look about to see if things are beginning to stick up out of the earth. I don't do any harm.'

'Don't look so frightened,' he said in a worried voice. 'You could not do any harm, a child like you! You may do what you like.'

Mary put her hand up to her throat because she was afraid he might see the excited lump which she felt jump into it. She was a step nearer.

'May I?' she asked nervously. Her anxious little face seemed to worry him more than ever.

'Don't look so frightened,' he exclaimed. 'Of course you may. I am your guardian, though I am a poor one for any child. I cannot give you time or attention; but I wish you to be happy and comfortable.'

'I don't know anything about children,' Mr Craven went on, 'but Mrs Medlock is to see that you have all you need.'

'May I have a bit of earth?' Mary asked in a tiny voice.

'A bit of earth?' Mr Craven was startled. 'What do you mean by a bit of earth?'

'To plant seeds in; to make things grow; to see them come alive,' Mary said.

'A bit of earth,' he said to himself, and Mary thought she must have reminded him of something. 'You can have as much earth as you want,' he said. 'You remind me of someone else who loved the earth and things that grow. When you see a bit of earth you want,' with something like a smile, 'take it, child, and make it come alive.'

'May I take it from anywhere—if it's allowed?'

'Anywhere,' he answered. 'But you must go now, I am tired. Goodbye, Mary. And I'd like to tell you that I shall be away again this summer.'

Then, she asked if she might visit Martha's home, and Mr Craven said she could.

Later that night, Mary again heard the mysterious child weeping. Defying Mrs Medlock's instructions, she went in search of the source of the sound and found that it came from a room in which the light was still burning. When she entered, she saw a pale, curious-looking boy lying in a large four-poster bed. He seemed to have

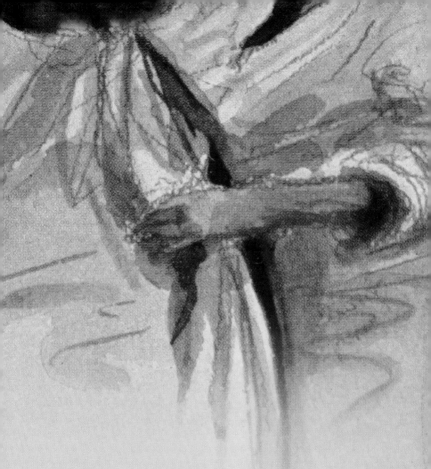

been ill for a long time. He introduced himself as Colin Craven, Mr Craven's son.

He said he was born just before his mother died. His father could not bear to see his wife's likeness in his son's eyes. Also, he was ashamed of how sickly the boy was. So he forbade his employees from talking about Colin. Everyone was afraid that Colin would turn into a hunchback, like his father, and die before he reached adulthood.

Colin did not like the attention he got wherever he went, and so stayed in the gloomy room all day. However, he was curious to know about Mary.

Mary was very glad to stay and talk to the sickly boy, in the hidden room for it reminded her a little of the secret garden. While the two of them were talking, Mary mentioned about the secret garden. This sparked Colin's interest. He wanted to know everything about the garden. He told Mary that his father and his servants would give him anything he wanted to amuse himself, since anger made him ill.

Gradually, Mary asked Colin why he had been crying. Colin said his doctor, who was also Mr Craven's brother, would inherit the manor if he, Colin, died. He said he wept because he had been thinking of his approaching death.

The boy then told Mary that he would love to see the garden, and that he would make the servants take him there. Mary explained that

the garden would not be secret if everyone knew where it was! Colin had never shared a secret with anyone but agreed to keep this one.

The next day, Mary told Martha that she met Colin and that he wished to see her every day. Although initially hesitant, Martha agreed to do whatever pleased the young Master Craven. Later, in his room, Mary told Colin that his attitude and anger towards others, especially the servants, was very unlike Dickon, who could charm people as well as animals. She told Colin how Dickon taught her to love the moor and that he might too, if he went outside.

Mary said that a visit from Dickon might help cheer Colin up and asked if she could arrange a meeting. Colin was thrilled by the idea. When they finally met, their laughter echoed through the passages, surprising everybody present there.

After a week of rain and Colin's constant company, Mary finally returned to the secret garden. She realized that Colin was not sick when he was engaged in some activity or conversation.

When Mary met Dickon in the garden, the two of them talked about Colin and discussed the growth of the plants. Mary explained her theory about keeping Colin busy. They also resolved to bring the latter to the secret garden. That way, Mary said, he could share the joy of watching the flowers bloom rather than sitting in a gloomy room, thinking about death all day long.

When she returned to the manor for lunch, Martha informed Mary that Colin had requested her company at once. She explained that it would not be possible right then, as Dickon was waiting for her outside. Colin was furious that Mary chose to spend her time with Dickon instead of him, leading to a heated argument between the two.

'Have you forgotten that I am ill and nearing my death?' Colin asked.

Mary scoffed at this. She told Colin that there was nothing wrong with him; he was just indulging in self-pity and stormed out of the room.

That night, Mary heard Colin weeping loudly. She was fearful at first, but soon grew tired and irritated at Colin's tantrums. One of the servants came to her room and asked Mary to scold him. So she burst into his room and told him that if he screamed one more time, she would scream louder than him and that would be scary. Shocked, Colin stopped crying immediately.

'I felt the lump on my back,' he said tearfully. 'I knew I was turning into a hunchback and I will soon be dead.'

'You felt nothing!' Mary said, annoyed.

'I did!'

'Nurse, come here and show me his back please,' she requested.

'Show her! Show her! Then she'll know!' said Colin.

When Mary saw the young boy's back, she began to laugh.

'There's nothing wrong with your back!' said Mary.

For the first time, Colin felt that his illness was largely a part of his own imagination. He said he would go out onto the moor if Mary and Dickon joined him.

The next day, Colin told the doctor about his planned excursion. The greedy doctor was not very pleased with the improvement in Colin's health since he wanted to inherit the manor.

He reminded Colin that he was very ill and told him not to exert himself too much. Colin replied that Mary's company made him forget about his illness which was also why he liked spending time with her.

The following morning, Mary opened the windows in Colin's room and instructed him to breathe the fresh air. She said Dickon often remarked that fresh air made him feel like he could live forever. Fascinated by this idea of good health, Colin insisted on going out. Dickon joined them after breakfast and the three children prepared for their visit to the secret garden.

Colin was adamant that the servants remained ignorant about the garden and so insisted that he would go out with only Mary and Dickon for company.

After he was dressed, a footman carried him out on his wheelchair. From there, Mary and Dickon took turns pushing the chair.

The lush greenery and clean air delighted Colin; the secret garden enchanted him. His pale skin began to take on a rosy glow in the bright sunlight and fresh air. He looked at Mary and Dickon and said, 'I could live forever and ever and ever!'

In the garden, Mary and Dickon showed him the various kinds of plants and flowers they had been growing.

Then, Colin asked about the tree from which his mother fell. The others did not want to answer and, luckily, Colin soon got distracted by the robin.

Dickon later told Colin that Mrs Sowerby felt that Mrs Craven was still in the garden in spirit, watching over her son. On hearing this, Colin said he wanted to go there every day.

Suddenly, the gardener appeared. He looked very angry but soon calmed down when he saw who was in the formerly locked garden. He was especially astonished to see Colin. When the children asked him to join them, he mellowed further. He said he visited the garden once every year to tend to the rose bushes. He informed the day because Mrs Craven's only request was that he take care of the roses she so dearly loved.

Back at the manor, Dr Craven visited Colin, who was very rude to him.

Mary was taken aback by his behaviour and scolded him. She reminded him that the only reason he had gotten his way was because people regarded him as a sick pitiable creature.

Mary's frankness astonished Colin. He told her he wished to get better and stop being known as the sick child. However, he wanted to keep his improving health a secret from everyone else in the manor for the time being, so that they could surprise Mr Craven when he returned from his trip.

Thereafter, the children would go out into the garden and sit cross-legged, and Colin would chant his desire to get better and healthier. They believed that the garden contained a mystical and magical force.

The three children had decided to tell Mrs Sowerby about their secret, and so every evening, Dickon told her about the day's happenings. Dickon also told her that they would keep pretending, so that no one found out about Colin's improving health.

The kind and affectionate Mrs Sowerby was amused by the children's revelation and promised to send them milk, potatoes and eggs. In the meantime, the children continued to harness the magical powers of the garden, while Colin's health improved significantly.

On rainy days, Mary and Colin were forced to stay indoors. So Mary suggested that they explore the numerous locked rooms. When they discovered the painting of the little girl with a parrot on her finger, Mary realized that she no longer looked like the girl in the portrait. She had been transformed by springtime and the healing powers of the garden. Mary also noticed that Colin had drawn aside the curtains in his room, revealing a portrait of his mother, which was previously hidden. Colin told her that his room was also filled with magic.

One day, Mary told Colin that he might be the representation of his mother's ghost. He was greatly moved by the possibility and thought to himself that his father might finally take a liking to him when he returned.

One afternoon, Ben the gardener commented on how healthy and well Colin looked; the boy responded saying that his experiments with magic had succeeded. He was so overwhelmed that he leapt up and declared that he would indeed live forever and ever and ever.

Suddenly, Mrs Sowerby entered the garden and was thrilled to see how strong and vigorous Colin appeared. She noted how closely he resembled his mother. She embraced him and Mary. Mrs Sowerby then told the group that Mr Craven would come home soon and see how wonderful things had become since his departure. Colin was touched and said he wished Mrs Sowerby were his mother.

'Your mother is always present here in the garden, lad!' Mrs Sowerby replied as she hugged him.

***

While sitting at his desk, Mr Craven found an unopened letter addressed to him. It read:

Dear Sir,

I am Susan Sowerby who talked to you boldly once on the moor. It was about Miss Mary I spoke. I will be bold to speak again. Please, sir, I would come home if I were you. I think you would be glad to come and— if you will excuse me, sir—I think your lady would ask you to come if she was here.

Your obedient servant,

Susan Sowerby.

Mr Craven immediately decided to leave for Misselthwaite Manor. On the way, he thought about his son and how he had neglected him. He was then overcome by a strong desire to mend his relationship with his son when he reached home.

When Mr Cravens returned to the manor, he stopped by Susan Sowerby's house to deliver the gifts he had brought for her children.

When he reached the manor, he enquired about Colin and Mary. Mrs Medlock told him that the children would be at the garden.

Mr Craven hurried to the garden and was astonished to see Colin and Mary laughing; he was delighted to see his son in such good health. He hugged his son and asked him to show him around the secret garden. Colin agreed, and told him how the secret garden was rediscovered and replenished. It was flourishing now. The three of them spent some time in the garden and returned to the manor, utterly amazed at Mr Craven's happiness and Colin's vigour now that it was no longer a secret.

Other Titles
In The Series

JUNIOR CLASSICS

Captains Courageous

The Ingenious Gentleman Don Quixote of La Mancha

The Man in the Iron Mask

The Red Badge of Courage

2

ABRIDGED AND ILLUSTRATED

JUNIOR CLASSICS

The Call of the Wild

Moby Dick or the Whale

The Little Mermaid

Animal Farm

1

ABRIDGED AND ILLUSTRATED

JUNIOR CLASSICS

Heidi

A Tale of Two Cities

Little Women

Black Beauty

4

ABRIDGED AND ILLUSTRATED

JUNIOR CLASSICS

Great Expectations

Around the World in Eighty Days

The Jungle Book

The Merry Adventures of Robin Hood

5

ABRIDGED AND ILLUSTRATED

JUNIOR CLASSICS

The Mutiny of the Bounty

The Adventures of Pinocchio

King Solomon's Mines

20,000 Leagues under the Sea

6

ABRIDGED AND ILLUSTRATED

JUNIOR CLASSICS

The Last of the Mohicans

The Legend of Sleepy Hollow

The Mayor of Casterbridge

The War of the Worlds

7

ABRIDGED AND ILLUSTRATED

JUNIOR CLASSICS

The Strange Case of Dr Jekyll and Mr Hyde

Frankenstein

The Invisible Man

Dracula

8

ABRIDGED AND ILLUSTRATED

JUNIOR CLASSICS

Pride and Prejudice

The Devoted Friend

The Gold Bug

The Mill on the Floss

9

ABRIDGED AND ILLUSTRATED

JUNIOR CLASSICS

Anne of Green Gables

Ivanhoe

The Enchanted Castle

The Hound of the Baskervilles

10

ABRIDGED AND ILLUSTRATED